CONTENTS

MONOLOGUES FOR STAGE

R.I.P MARIA CALLAS	3
THE STANDARD BEARER	19
THE LIMO FROM HELL	37

MONOLOGUES FOR RADIO

TINKLING THE IVORIES	53
THE ICEMAN RETURNETH	63
HO! HO! HO!	73
SOUR BEER	83

Copyright Stephen Wyatt
All rights are reserved.
Any enquiries regarding performance or reproduction should be addressed to the author's agents, Valerie Hoskins Associates, 20 Charlotte Street, London W1P IHJ. Telephone: (020) 76374490.

ISBN 978-0-9556868-0-1

R.I.P. MARIA CALLAS

First performed by Richard Albrecht
at the Edinburgh Festival and subsequently at the Hen and
Chickens, London.
1992.

Directed by Sue Dunderdale

(David, a man in his late thirties, sits on a pub stool.)
(After a short silence he speaks.)

I used to sit here in this pub. At the start of the evening, I ordered my usual five double whiskies. Why? Because I know by the time I had consumed the first four, I would be incapable of moving from the stool to get any more.

Pause.

I would be interesting to find out how many people ever registered my presence. Not in a "Gosh, good lord, it's old Dave, great to see you, mate" sense. But registered in the sense of being aware how often I secreted myself away in this little nook. God knows why I selected this bar. I suppose it has a certain faded charm. A sense of former glories mot quite turned to plastic lampshades and flock wall-paper. A barmaid whose manner is neither gushing nor surly. A carpet of nondescript colour and pattern so that one could stare fixedly at it without one's head going round and round. A sense of pleasing emptiness.

Pause.

When I was drunk enough, I'd bore people to death about the merits of Maria Callas compared with those of Joan Sutherland and Monserrat Caballe – not to mention more recent aspirants to Callas's vocal throne. I was an opera buff, you see. For 'buff' you may choose to read 'bore'. (PAUSE) Some people seem to think there is something endearing about the conversation of heavy drinkers. I don't see it myself. However brilliant or revealing their conversation, there's a loop in the tape. Certain ideas won't go away.

Pause. He goes into a mock documentary voice.

On the outskirts of this town of ours stands a small Victorian Gothic brick building of limited architectural merit. It has, however, a deeply useful function to perform. It is a corporation urinal. No different from countless others up and down the country. Even the graffiti are standards. References to the triumphs of local football teams and racist remarks of horrendous bigotry. Nothing special you might think. But you would be wrong.

He provides hummed suspense music.

Dum da dum dum dum. If you outside this place late at night, even in these enlightened times, you would observe a remarkably large number of men entering and leaving the male end of the convenience, marked, in memory of older and more spacious days, 'Gentlemen'. But what makes these men leave the warmth and comfort of their own homes to wander aimlessly around this bleak public urinal? Surely it cannot be its architectural delights or the charm of its views? Surely not all these wanderers of the night can suffer from uncontrollably weak bladders? Surely they cannot all be earnest students of the current state of the Milky Way? And if from the profusion of tight cycling shorts, you deduced that they all members of a cycling club, then where are the bicycles? Something odd is clearly going on as they peer earnestly through the gloom at each other, looking back over their shoulders as they pass. Young and old, well to do and out of work, leather clad and dressed in tweed, they all share one dark secret. This is not a story for the squeamish. You have been warned. Dum da dum dum –

He suddenly breaks off.

The man who's just come in spoke to me once. As a public-spirited citizen, he attempted to help me up when I toppled off my stool. For my pains, he received my rendition of the Mad Scene from Lucia di Lammermoor full belt. I think it startled him a little. In any case he never spoke to me again.

Pause.

I worked in the Borough Planning Department. I used to say that the pay wasn't bad and the work was pleasant enough – and people used to say, "That sounds like faint praise." Which, of course, it was. There was only one real justification for going through those absurd motions day by day. Money. Believe it or not, I was rather good at the job. They kept on promoting me. Which increased not decreased my detachment from the proceedings. I couldn't believe nobody noticed by apparently they didn't. Maybe they were all playing the same game. I had a fantasy. A fantasy! This was one of my fantasies. That's better. One day in the office my eyes would meet those of my colleagues. A glint in my eyes. A glint in theirs. Then we all start giggling, quietly at first but with increasing volume. The madness would spread. One by one each inmate of the Planning Department would collapse in hysterics. We would be rolling about on the floor helpless with laughter at the absurdity of it all.

Pause.

It won't surprise you to learn it never happened. We sat each day, our brows dutifully furrowed in fake concern, getting on with the weighty business of making decisions that were never implemented and preparing plans that ended up in the litter bin. Once I tried. There was a beautiful late Georgian street called Blithesdale Terrace. I was very fond of it. They were going to build flats here but they ran out of money. So it's currently a less than beautiful heap of rubble. After that I decided it was best not to bother. Multi-storey car parks and out-of-town shopping centre shall, it seems, inherit the earth.

Pause.

I got on well enough with my colleagues. I cherish the illusion that I was not generally loathed. The tea lady even quite liked me. But, in any case, all cordialities ceased on the dot of five-thirty. My flat remained a sanctum penetrated by few. Though, it has to be said, the privilege was not widely sought after. Particularly in the last few years.

Pause.

There's a certain etiquette to the thing. An ideal subject for the budding sociologist. Or perhaps anthropologist. There's certainly a strong ritualistic element. Dark primeval deeds performed at the dead of night. For the true devotee, a brightly lit urinal is something to be shunned. The craving is for gloom – and obscurity. On entry – assuming he's not actually following someone else in – the new acolyte allows a few seconds to accustom his eyes to the situation. Here a tell-tale groping tells of activity already under way. There an exchange of glances indicates the beginning of interest. There a sudden movement away indicates that a tiny drama of courtship has ended in brutal rejection by one of the participants. A whole pageant of human emotion and sexual desire played in total silence, the darkness perhaps occasionally illuminated by the lighting of a cigarette.

Pause.

Oddly, for most addicts, physical satisfaction is not a sine qua non. There is the pleasure of the chase. And the exhilarating scent of degradation and danger mingling with other more tangible odours.

Pause.

I have always been of the opinion that Maria Callas had more talent in her little finger than Joan Sutherland has in the whole of her body. Joanie has a superb voice but not one ounce of dramatic feeling. I am being unfair. She is a highly talented artiste. But not as talented as Callas. No way.

Pause.

I nearly started singing bits of Traviata to prove it. 'Gran Dio! Morir si giovane' and all that. Callas understood about dying you, you see. Whereas Joanie is still with us.

Pause.

The curious thing about my particular little incident is that to this day I have no clear idea of what the other person looked like. The shape seemed reassuring and even refined in the gloom but that is all I can say. There is an etiquette to the whole thing but that doesn't include formal introductions.

Pause.

A light flashes suddenly in the darkness. Before he knows what has happened, the unsuspecting victim is bundled outside. He is bewildered, blinking in disbelief. He is dimly aware that the area is suddenly vacant. The others are nowhere in sight. He is well and truly alone. And the questions come thick and fast. Name. Age. Address. Occupation. Intentions.

Pause.

I suppose one could appreciate the grotesque comedy. My attempts to pass myself off as a fresh air friend enjoying a late night ramble were soon put pay to. They had seen me entering and re-entering the aforesaid cottage some eight times over the period of an hour. Such is the devotion and meticulousness of the police in the execution of their duty. A more interesting discussion took place over the state of my penis at the time of arrest and whether or not it could have been accurately described as erect. In the end one realised that to argue longer was to court greater retribution.

Pause. He switches into a policeman's voice in the cosy style of 'Dixon of Dock Green'.

And so another busy night for the police nears its end. Honest citizens can sleep safer in their beds knowing that sexual perverts aren't up to any hanky-panky down at the local convenience. Not that we like getting mixed up in this sort of thing, of course. Some of our lads run quite a risk when they go in there in mufti. Still, it's all worth while in the end, isn't it? So good night and remember, the next time you see a pouf, spit in his eye. 'Night all.

He starts to whistle the 'Dixon of Dock Green' theme then stops.

One of the great tragedies of my life is never having seen Maria Callas on stage. In my flat you'd find virtually every recording ever made of her, however appalling the quality of reproduction. They're all amazing – even the ones made when she didn't have any voice left. She should never have tried to lose weight. She ended up looking fantastic but her voice was never the same again. Understandable, I suppose. She was chasing after that bastard Aristotle Onassis. Or whatever. I just wish they hadn't dredged up all that about her life. What does it matter that she had an abortion at the age of forty three or whatever it was? Poor cow, let her be.

Pause.

I was a first offender. I looked terribly respectable and said I was deeply ashamed of what I'd done and would never do it again. The first statement was far truer than the second. I was fined a few quid. I found an excuse to get off work. The incident wasn't reported – why should it be? You could say that I got off rather lightly – on that occasion at least. Retribution bided its time. But I still remember how strange it was standing there in court. The activities described seemed to have nothing whatsoever to do with me. The policeman giving evidence could have been reading bits out of the News of the World. He certainly didn't seem to be describing my ludicrous arrest in flagrante, hastily doing up my flies and trying not to panic. Is there any more ludicrous image to be haunted by? For months after, I used to try and rewrite the script so that my replies were not quite so grovellingly inept and my panic more adequately restrained. Perhaps I should have denied everything or made a run for it. Anything would have been preferable to what I did.

Pause.

Never look back. What a fatuous saying. How would people sitting alone in pubs ever pass the time if they didn't look back?

Pause.

I surprised myself when all the dirt about Callas started coming out in the wonderful Sunday supplement way it always does. I thought I was going to be all agawp for juicy titbits and I ended up feeling slightly sick. I had to stop reading and put on one of her records instead. Somehow it seemed the decent thing to do. Why, I wonder, does one get so indignant about things that have nothing to do with one personally? She's past caring, isn't she? Besides, she's not the only person who's wanted to be beautiful and loved and successful. You could say she was lucky to manage two out of three at the same time. Some of us don't manage any. And she left us the recordings. Above all, La Traviata...

David starts to sing quietly but with growing intensity.

Gran Dio! Morir si giovane,
Io che penato ho tanto!
Morir si presso a tergere
Il mio si lungo pianto…

<u>David's singing trails off.</u>

When I used to do that, it was generally in an undertone. Even so people used to edge away discreetly. Now I can sing out to my heart's content.

<u>He sings the opening louder.</u>

You may have noticed that I keep saying 'I used to…' That is, of course, because I am dead.

<u>Pause.</u>

It's changed things. I don't just mean becoming dead but what went before. Getting ill, I mean. Really ill.

<u>Pause. He hums the opening phrase of 'Morir si giovane' again.</u>
<u>Pause.</u>

An international opera house is one of the last places you can still go and get a real sense of occasion. It is an event, right from the outrageous price you have to pay for the tickets and the programme. As the lights are dimmed, a round of applause greets the conductor. There is a final burst of coughing and rustling of programmes and then, as he raises his baton, total silence. The singers still behave with a flamboyance and extravagance nobody would dare to employ anywhere else. People declare undying love for each other at considerable length without so much as a glance in each other's direction. Overweight tenors attempts swordfights of a geriatric character and large sopranos clamber uneasily over cut-out rocks. All the time, however, you are wallowing in the most beautiful sounds.

And at the end, to cap the event, the curtain calls. They can go on and on. First the chorus. Then the chorus and the principals. Then the leading lady brings on the conductor. The conductor gestures towards the orchestra, most of who have gone home by this point. Then the principal calls one by one. The women get bouquets from flunkies. Everybody bows and curtsies ad infinitum. The audience cheer and throw flowers or boo as the mood takes them. Nothing like that ever happens to the Queen any more. I used to love it. You can't get an atmosphere like that anywhere else. Well, you certainly can't get it in the Borough Planning Department.

Pause.

I remember I took Paul once. The opera was Norma. He said it was quite pleasant but he couldn't really get all that excited about it. I think he felt rather the same about me. Retrospectively, it was a mistake. Not going to Norma, I mean, even though it was with Joanie, but getting into conversation in the first place and inviting him back to the flat. You just don't do that sort of thing. Getting to know other people is a sentimental luxury. The bushes are quite sufficient for anything you really have to say – or do – to each other. Still, one learns by one's mistakes. Well, actually, maybe not. Maybe that was where all the trouble started. I have rather suspected it was.

Pause.

As a mater of fact, I used to think I'd got it all worked out rather neatly – compared with my colleagues whose social lives, families, hobbies and jobs merged messily one into the other. Being a very tidy person, I got pleasure out of the separateness of the compartments. The work used to give me money, the opera used to give me imagination, extravagance and colour, and the covert sex used to give me, well, covert sex.

Pause.

I never told anybody when I was diagnosed. My work colleagues were just that. And it was hardly a matter you'd discuss with a fellow opera buff over a gin and tonic in the interval of Cosi Fan Tutte. Let alone with your trousers down at the dead of night behind a bush. But I did my best to be sexually responsible, I really did. After all, I'd promised Brenda.

Pause.

Or was it Sheila? It was certainly something Australian. She was the counsellor at the clinic and she made me discuss my future – or lack of it. Well, 'discuss' is probably not the right word. There was hardly a meeting of minds. She was from the New World, frank, jolly, open, called a spade a spade and encouraged others to do the same, a fresh of fresh air in an inhibited guilt-ridden world. So you can see why I loathed her on sight.

Pause.

Still, a promise is a promise. And otherwise I carried on as if nothing had happened. Which for some time wasn't that difficult as nothing much did happen.

Pause.

After Callas lost weight, she appeared in a new production of Rossini's Il Turco in Italia. She didn't like her costumes. "All that dieting and you give me a waistline right up here," she complained. "Nobody will see how slim I am." She kept on secretly getting the seamstress to alter them. And the director, just as secretly, got the altered back. (Pause.) Do you know who she really wanted to look like, that dark, plump Greek woman? You can see it very clearly in the offstage photos. She was trying to be Audrey Hepburn.

Pause.

I have a horror of groups of people. I hate to be identified as one of a kind, even a Borough Planner. Though, in view of what we've done to our particular Borough, that's a wise decision. But when things got out of control, when I finally got sick, I mean really 'sick' in inverted commas, there was only one group that I could look to for support in matters unmedical. There comes a point when you realise your plan to claim to have acquired a rare South American disease founders on he fact that not only have you never been near South America, you've never knowingly met a South American. Colleagues can be fobbed off for a considerable length of time, parents wilfully mislead but ultimately, alas, you have to talk to someone.

Pause.

Damian once asked me if there was any limit to my fascination with opera. And I said yes, there was. I don't have sexual fantasies about Luciano Pavarotti.

Pause.

I'm not good at groups, as I said. It was like Brenda multiplied. Or Sheila multiplied as the case may be. The smiles, the frankness, the camaraderie. It felt like I was back at a Sunday School Christmas Party. I had to introduce myself – stand up and say who I was and what I was – to a motley selection of people, mostly male, mostly perverts. I was tempted to lie wildly. But life isn't like that, is it? Just when you need a string of convenient whoppers, your mind goes completely blank and you end up delivering something embarrassingly close to the truth.

Pause.

I think, on the whole, it was a more humiliating experience than being arrested by the police. Still, everyone persisted in being kind and understanding and welcoming and all that. And things did improve later. I discovered that all these wonderful caring people could also be petty-minded, bad-tempered, egocentric and just plain boring. Which was an enormous relief. Some of them were also quite interesting. Well, Damian was, anyway,

<u>Pause</u>.

The operatic stage is not an ideal preparation for real life, Consumption was an unpleasant way to die but I don't recall a production of La Traviata where Violetta was on anything like a drip – or expired in a mass of soiled bed sheets. Death in opera is, well, musical.

<u>Pause</u>.

I had always imagined that I would get through my entire life without meeting anyone called Damian. But this particular Damian was hard to miss. He was very pale and painfully thin with studs through his nose and a T-short that said 'Queer as Fuck'. I am not describing a great passion here. Not even a crush. Just an interesting exchange of opinions. Damian explained to me that we weren't 'gay' any more, we were 'queer'. That was because we were uncompromising and angry now about the way we had been treated and wouldn't take any more nonsense. I tried to explain that I'd only just got round to thinking of myself as 'gay' so this was rather a lot to take on, But he was very sweet about it. He called it a generation gap. I think it was a meeting of irreconcilable value systems.

<u>Pause</u>.

Perversely, I both resented the fact that I felt identified and classified as something called 'gay' – or possibly 'queer' – and the fact that the organisation helped people who weren't gay at all. Still, I suppose it enabled me to go on fudging the issue with parents and colleagues for a while longer.

Pause.

Damien never gave up trying though. He explained about Gay Pride marches, Clause 28, the club scene, who was or wasn't one of us in tennis, football, TV soaps, pop music, the Hollywood musical, cricket, athletics, the Church of England, the Inland Revenue, the Conservative Party… I think it have him a real thrill to find somebody as deeply ignorant as I was.

Pause.

I tried to reciprocate. I told him about the largest voice I'd ever heard on the operatic stage – Birgit Nilsson's. I'd read somewhere that if Birgit Nilsson stood close to a grand piano and expanded her diaphragm, just expanded her diaphragm, the piano would start to move, The piano was on casters, of course, but all the same…

Pause.

There is no doubt that Damien's death was far less melodic and formally satisfying than that of Violetta or Mimi but it had, I think, a certain dignity. I wasn't there in a leading role, of course. Somebody else was the tenor flinging himself flamboyantly across the deathbed, I was just there as a comprimario – a faithful servant, perhaps, just a few lines of recitative and a supporting role in the final ensemble.

Pause.

Violetta in Traviata was Maria Class's greatest role. Consider the story. A woman in a man's world earns her not insubstantial crust by selling her body. She falls in love with Alfredo, gives it all up and foes to live with him in the country – on <u>her</u> money. Enter Alfredo's father who persuades Violetta to give up her lover so that his innocent young sister's marriage can go ahead. Violetta convinced that nothing lasts anyway agrees to comply with the old bastard's ludicrous demand. She gives up Alfredo and goes back to her old life. Unaware of her painful sacrifice, Alfredo viciously humiliates her. Eventually, of course, everything is sorted out – Alfredo discovers the truth, he apologises and they realise that he really loves her and she really loves him et cetera et cetera. Unfortunately, by this point, Violetta is dying so it's all too late. End of opera.

<u>Pause.</u>

Maria callas died alone in her Paris flat. She was on so many pills by that time, pills to wake her up, pills to put her to sleep, that it's a technicality deciding whether she consciously committed suicide or not. But I'm afraid I like to believe that she too went out to the sound of one of her own recordings. Preferably, of course, La Traviata.

<u>Pause.</u>

The odd thing about Maria Callas is that for all her flamboyance and her temperament and her tantrums, she was a victim. All her life she let men walk all over her and all the love and devotion pouring out of her fans didn't ever make her feel confident and good about herself.

<u>Pause.</u>

I can't help feeling she'd have lasted longer and better if she'd got angry. I don't mean, lost her temper and screamed a lot. She did quite a bit of that anyway. I mean, really, deep down, angry.

Pause. We hear Callas singing 'La Traviata'…

But angry about what exactly? And, come to that, with whom?

Pause. Lights fade.
Callas's voice fades away.

End.

THE STANDARD BEARER

First performed by David Gant
at the Man in the Moon Theatre, London.
2001.

Directed by Jane Paton

West Africa. 1980.
A table with a carafe of water and a glass. A chair.
GEORGE, an actor in his late fifties, enters, quite showily dressed with some concessions towards the tropical clime he is currently visiting.

Ladies and gentlemen, boys and girls, the natural instincts of an old trouper on an occasion like this are for plunging straight in. But for several reasons, some pleasant, some not so pleasant, that is not possible this evening. Let us take the pleasant first. I must thank your Headmaster and his Board of Governors for making available to us this charming little hall. To be honest, we hadn't known quite what to expect and so this has proved a most pleasant surprise. Really. Our thanks also must go to his Excellency, the Minister for Cultural and Educational Affairs who has been instrumental in arranging our tour and has sent us on a journey of discovery far more wide-ranging and exciting than we had ever imagined when we first started to plan this visit. Finally, thanks to you all for the warmth of your welcome – and also for your patience. Which brings me inevitably to the less pleasant reasons. I must apologise profusely on behalf of my wife and myself for keeping you all waiting so long, through, I fear, no fault of our own. The British Cultural Representative here in your country, Sandy, is in many ways a sterling fellow. But, alas, he has rather an optimistic view of distances through the bush once one is away from the capital, where, inevitably, he spends nearly all his time. As a result, you have been kept waiting and we have had a rather frantic and unsettling journey. Indeed, I'm not sure that we would have made it at all had it not been for the efforts of our driver/stage manager, Tim. (He gestures briefly towards the wings.) Now, nothing makes me more uncomfortable than having to maunder on in this fashion particularly as I'm aware that some of you have come considerable distances on foot to see what we have to show you of England's greatest dramatist and the plays you have been studying for exams.

I too would like to be up and doing if – Excuse me just a moment.

<u>He stops and goes to the wings.</u>

Tim, any sign of - (<u>Clearly receiving a thumbs down</u>) Oh. Oh well. Ladies and gentlemen, the unfortunate fact is that my wife, Enid, my partner in tonight's programme as in many earlier theatrical collaborations, has been left somewhat indisposed by our lengthy journey and is therefore not able to join me immediately up here. There's no cause for concern – I've no doubt she will have recovered in a few minutes and will then be able to join me in those passages where two voices are undoubtedly better than one. But inevitably this has involved some reorganisation of our programme of extracts and anecdote, which I hope will not seriously incommode the students among you. My offer to cancel tonight and try again tomorrow was refused with the most flattering insistence and indeed I suppose it is scarcely likely that many of you could make a similar journey again so soon. But enough – at last – of preamble – let us set the scene – (<u>He stops and talks to the wings in a half-whisper:</u>) Tim, Tim, I know we need that generator going for obvious reasons but am I alone in finding those fans rather loud. (<u>Listens</u>) Oh, oh, I see. I hadn't appreciated how far they were needed not only for coolness but to deter the little creatures of the night. We'll have to manage. (<u>To audience :</u>) So without more ado.

<u>He turns a makes a gesture. A tinny recorded fanfare issues from an age old recorder. As it plays, GEORGE sits, mops his brow and takes a long drink from the carafe.</u>
<u>As the fanfare music concludes, he rises dramatically and delivers the Prologue from</u> **Henry V**:

>O for a muse of fire, that would ascend
>The brightest heaven of invention:
>A kingdom for a stage, princes to act,

And monarchs to behold the swelling scene.
Then should the warlike Harry, like himself
Assume the port of Mars, and at his heels,
Leashed in like hounds, should famine, sword and fire
Crouch for employment. But pardon, gentles all,
The flat unraised spirits that hath dared
On this unworthy scaffold to bring forth
So great an object...
O pardon: since a crooked figure may
Attest in little place a million
And let us, ciphers to this great account,
On your imaginary forces work...
Piece out our imperfections with your thoughts...
Think, when we talk of horses, that you see them,
Printing their proud hoofs i'th' receiving earth;
For 'tis your thoughts that now must deck our kings,
Carry them here and there, jumping o'er times,
Turning the accomplishment of many years
Into an hourglass...

George stops and takes a drink, mops his brow.

Now I stand before you on a bare stage with nothing before me but a chair, a table and – a carafe of water. Not that far from the 'wooden o' where the Chorus in Shakespeare's Henry V stood some four hundred years ago and, like me, tried to compel his audience's attention by describing things they weren't actually going to see. Not a cheat, of course, but part of the essence of the actor's art. "The accomplishment of many years" too. How vividly that phrase convets the concentration and intensity of the dramatic art, where within the scope of a single evening the course of a character's whole life may be mapped out – from early manhood and marriage to senility and death. Indeed –

He stops and looks expectantly into the wings.

I thought she was just coming. Ah, well. Anyway, to continue. Here tonight we return to some of the conventions that made Shakespeare's own theatre. We are travelling players, taking our wares – as much as can be packed into a Landrover, no more – wherever in West Africa there is a hunger for Shakespeare's work. And I noticed tonight as I recited to you, the gratifying hum of your voices repeating the lines with me as I declaimed them. And perhaps I should further explain, since my wife still appears to be indisposed, this is a journey that has a very personal meaning for my wife and myself. A sentimental journey in fact. Sometimes time passes in our own lives with a swiftness we can barely credit, and in a way that is as miraculous as anything that happens on stage. (Drinking) Or as Shakespeare said in another place, thus the whirligig of time brings in his revenges. Allow me to illustrate.

Pause.

My grandfather was also a distinguished actor – though obviously you couldn't be expected to know that. He visited Africa several times during his lifetime and performed a number of Shakespeare plays along with what were then regarded as the prime examples of the West End stage at its best – works now lost in the mists of time with titles like The Sign of the Cross and Nell of Old Drury. Perhaps his pioneering spirit still lingers on dimly in me. He came here first in 1903 just after the end of the Boer War and a couple of times after that before our own Great War in Europe. Of course he was touring in – in the bottom part of Africa, the other bit... But the point I want to mak is this. He brought his own company over with him from England. None of this whipping over by plane, it took four weeks by boat. Each time he brought five production. And – this is the point I'm really making since I've seen the records – for these productions my grandfather brought with hin on that sea voyage and on the trains over here or whatever else was going to travel around the bit down there – he brought a company of twenty-seven actors, plus a backstage staff of eight including stage managers, costumiers and a resident scene-painter, plus seventeen skips of costume and properties, twenty three pairs of flats, thirty-five assorted rostra and twenty-sox different painted backcloths. Whereas we – are as you see.

Pause. He drinks.

Well, I suppose you could look at that in one of two ways. Firstly, excuse the French, how bloody magnificent. Not an ounce of subsidy. All my grandfather's own money raised from stomping the provinces, even doing the odd bit of Hamlet in some of the classier music halls, and all of it likely as not oing down the drain. The first time he'd never been to Africa and there were no Sandoes running around to set things up for him. And he made a packet. Which unfortunately he lost on the second tour. But that's not my main point. (To wings:) Yes, yes, Tim, I know, I'm gettoing there. (Back to audience:) There is another way of looking at it. What did he need all that stuff for? Shakespeare didn't need it down the Globe so why did he? Let us return to those Shakespearean virtues of evocation and economy. Please piece out our imperfections with your thoughts. Excuse me, the heat.

Pause. He drinks.

Ah yes, the hourglass. In the words of that rather more modern English playwright, Mr. J.B.Priestley, we have been here before. And have very happy memories. Sometime during the 1950s – when Britannia still ruled the waves around here as it were – and we were what was known then rather grandly as juvenile leads, we came to your capital in a production of – of all things – Noel Coward's Private Lives. We played Victor and Sybil, the parts generally referred to as the 'other parts' but not bad experience for a young actor and actress. We had hardly met before the rehearsals started. At the end of the play we were supposed to have a violent quarrel. I called here a "malicious little vixen" and she slapped me in the face. We fell in love. Here in your capital. We've always vowed that one day we would come back and now, somewhat longer in the tooth, that is what we have done.

He glances towards the wings but there's no response. He drinks.

On that occasion too, I recollect, the company brought its own set and costumes. Albeit for a modest single production with a cast of five and borrowed furniture when we got there. We played, of course, in the Victoria Theatre and packed the place out. But then with all the British officials and their wives there was obviously quite a market for Coward and Lonsdale and Rattigan and – (His voice trails away) - all those english dramatists you couldn't possibly be expected to have heard of. Fogive me but it was a magical time. For us, at least. No doubt you feel much less sense of loss for those loud braying officials with their cocktail parties and games of squash. Now you have Sandy. (Pause.) I must, however, say, as I have already said to the Minister, that it seems a great pity that the Victoria Theatre has been allowed to fall into such disrepair. The plush is gone. The plasterwork drops off. The stage machinery such as it is rusts away. And goats appear to inhabit the auditorium. It was quite a shock to see it. And though it is probably impertinent of me to say so, I feel it is a mistake to let it rot away. We should all hold on to our cultural landmarks, however alien they may seem to be. Your Preseident was, after all, often to be seen in the stalls, having, I recall, a particular fondness for The Last of Mrs. Cheyney.

A comment from the wing.

Yes, yes I know. Let us return to a play close to my heart and, I believe, committed by many of you to memory.

Perhaps the most famous speech of all from Henry V. It needs only the words of setting Shakespeare gives us. "Enter the King, Exeter, Bedford and Gloucester. Alarum." (He makes a cueing gesture) Thank you, Tim. (Cod crowd noises and trumpet calls issue from the speaker. GEORGE announces over this:) "Enter Soldiers carrying scaling ladders at Harfleur." Thank you.

The noises continue while GEORGE takes a drink and possibly assumes a crown or producves a sword to wave. When he's ready, he makes another gesture. The crowd noises start to fade as he launches into Act Three Scene One of **Henry V.**

> Once more unto the breach, dear friends, once more'
> Or close the wall up with our English dead.
> In peace there's nothing so becomes a man
> As modest stillness and humility,
> But when the blast of war blows in our ears,
> Then imitate the action of the tiger.
> Stiffen the sinews, conjure up the blood,
> Disguise fair nature with hard-favoured rage…
> Hold hard the breath, and bend up every spirit
> To his full height. On, on, you noblest English…
> Dishonour not your mothers; now attest
> That those who you called father did beget you.
> Be copy now to men of grosser blood
> And teach them how to war! …
> For there is none of you so mean and base
> That hath not noble lustre in your eyes.
> I see you stand like greyhounds in the slips,
> Straining upon the start. The game's afoot.
> Follow your spirit and upon this charge
> Cry, 'God for Harry, England and Saint George!'

How glad I am that the examination board has seen fit to put this play on the syllabus (Removing crown etc.) And how much I would like to have heard my grandfather's rendering of that speech. The rallying to arms, firm, unboastful, dignified and yet stirring, inflammatory even. They have tried once and they have failed so he must persuade them to try again. With an appeal to patriotism that still stirs the blood. Sir Laurence Olivier – Larry – made a marvellous film of it during the war – the Second World War that is. But somehow these days back home the spirit doesn't seem to be around. And when somebody does try to make that sort of patriotic appeal, it all ends up sounding rather petty.

He drinks.

The heat, you understand. Forgive me, but this is something I feel strongly about. And I want to urge you, all of you, in this new nation you are building to hold on to your pride in what you have. As a matter of fact, I'm reminded of my only face to face meeting with your President. Of course, he wasn't your President then – and, come to think of it, I don't actually think he's your President now. But anyway, at that time his period as President was still to be. And we met at a garden party held at the Governor's palace, which was when I learned about his passion for Frederick Lonsdale. And he was very charming, beautifully dressed and we chatted for a while and had a few laughs. And, you know, a few months before I met him, he'd been put in prison by our lot for stirring up trouble, I'm sorry to say. And there he was, smiling and chatting, as if nothing had happened and all our diplomats were being terribly smooth and charming in return. And then a few months after that, there were disturbances somewhere or other and he was packed off back to jail. Enough to discourage anyone I would say. I mean, I can remember at the garden party some quite high-ranking British official telling me the African nationalists hadn't got a hope. And I don't think it was all that long after that –

Sandy after all gave us quite a careful briefing on all this so I should remember – nine months or a year or so, everything was changed. The British were packing their bags and preparing to leave and he was on his way to becoming your President. That is the power, I suppose, of really caring for your country. Once more unto the breach indeed.

He turns to the wings:

Tim – go and see where she is. (Listens) I don't remember Sandy having said anything about that. Of course they know who he is. Anyway, does it matter whether he was assassinated or not? Go and get Enid.

Pause. He drinks.

You are all being patient, most patient, but I think the time has come for us to move on to the major part of our programme, the presentation of selected scenes from your other main set book, Macbeth. For this, clearly, I shall need the assistance of my wife who by now should, should, be fully recovered.

He pauses expectantly. Nothing happens.

You know, English actors have their own very strange superstitions. Our very own voodoo. And Macbeth, otherwise known as 'the Scottish play' lies at the centre of many of them. Performances of the play are believed to be unusually prone to cancellations, disaster and deaths. It is also believed that it is very bad luck to quote a line from the play or mention its title in rehearsal or more particularly offstage in your dressing room. Various elaborate and rather absurd rituals are required to avert this bad luck if such things happen accidentally or thoughtlessly. So absurd are the rituals I will not reveal them to you. (Pause) Let us just hope the curse of Macbeth is not in operation tonight.

<u>Pause. He turns to the wings.</u>

Tim, where is she? She said just a few minutes. I can't go on like this much longer. I'm losing them. (<u>Listens</u>) No, I think she just wants to make a fool of me. Because of - Never mind, never mind. Just get her here.

<u>Pause. He turns back to the audience.</u>

One more thought. A respected general urged on by his wife murders the legitimate ruler of his country and seizes power. To hold on to that power he has to go on murdering the opposition until finally they get together enough forces to defeat and kill him. A blank verse tragedy written, what, nearly four hundred years ago? I don't mind telling you my wife and I had some pretty nasty moments when we considered performing it in certain territories not a million miles from here that it would not be tactful to name. You understand me.

<u>He drinks.</u>

Sandy hates me saying things like that. (<u>Pause</u>) Oh, where is the bloody woman? Tim, Tim – (<u>He turns to the wings</u>) What do you mean, she's not coming? We're professionals. At least I am and I thought she was. It's an act, isn't it – and don't start taking her side again. (<u>Pause</u>) Very well. So be it. (<u>Pause. He takes a long drink.</u>) A little water clears us of this deed. (<u>Pause</u>) Ladies and gentlemen, I shall now perform the murder scene from Shakespeare's <u>Macbeth</u>.

<u>GEORGE launches into the scene with great panache, stage directions and all, alternating between the two parts, only gradually losing conviction.</u>

	'Enter LADY MACBETH.'
LADY M:	That which hath made them drunk hath made me bold.

What hath quenched them hath given me fire. Hark, peace! ...
Alack, I am afraid they have awaked
And 'tis not done. Th'attempt and not the deed
Confounds us. Hark! – I laid their daggers ready;
He could not miss 'em. Had he not resembled
My father as he slept, I had done't.

'Enter MACBETH'

LADY M:	My husband!
MACBETH:	I have done the deed. Didst thou not hear a noise?
LADY M:	I heard the owl scream and the crickets cry.
	Did you not speak?
MACBETH:	When?
LADY M:	Now.
MACBETH:	As I descended?
LADY M:	Ay ...
MACBETH:	There's one did laugh in's sleep, and one cried 'Murder!'
	That they did wake each other. I stood and heard then.
	But they did say their prayers and addressed them
	Again to sleep...
	List'ning their fear I could not say 'Amen'
	When they did say 'God bless us.'
LADY M:	Consider it not so deeply.
MACBETH:	But wherefore could not I pronounce 'Amen'?
	I had most need of blessing, and 'Amen' Stuck in my throat.
LADY M:	These deeds must not be thought

	After these ways. So, it will make us mad.
MACBETH:	Methought I heard a voice cry 'Sleep no more,
	Macbeth doth murder sleep' – the innocent sleep,
	Sleep that knits up the ravelled sleave of care,
	The death of each day's life, sore labour's bath,
	Balm of hurt minds, great nature's second course,
	Chief nourisher in life's feast –
LADY M:	What do you mean?

<u>This last line is finally too much for him and he breaks off angrily.</u>

Oh, this is ludicrous, ludicrous. I won't go on with it. How dare she do this to me? How dare she?

<u>Pause.</u>

Thirty years. That is how long we have been married. All because of a very passionate, very beautiful idyll here in your country all that time ago. Everyone said how well we were suited as a couple. And how lucky we are to have found so many opportunities to act together. That first physical attraction which happened just a few hundred miles from here was extraordinary, overwhelming. So we married. And in good time several children ensued.

<u>Pause. He drinks.</u>

However ludicrous, it may seem, this tour was planned not to celebrate our marriage but to save it. Somewhere inside us for some inconceivable reason we believed that the hatred, the bile, the disgust, the boredom we now feel for each other, and for the country we belong to, might somehow here miraculously disappear. Our friends told us we were mad. Why struggle any more? Why not just let each other be, divorce if you must, live separate lives, you're old enough, aren't you? Why this? Why that? They kept on asking relentlessly. And the truth is that somewhere, deep down, amidst all that venom and hatred and habit, we are still in love. Still. I wish to God it would go away but it does not. And I know why Enid came here and she knows why I came.

<u>Pause. Then very loudly:</u>

Tim, please, switch those bloody fans off.

<u>Pause. He drinks.</u>

And let's be bloody frank about this. It's been bloody awful since we arrived. Not made any easier by that twerp of a Sandy who couldn't organise his way out of a paper bag. Or by having to travel millions of miles across the bloody bush because there aren't any decent theatres any more. We must have been bloody mad. Bloody mad. Ask me why we're here and I don't know any more. We were supposed to recapture something. (<u>Pause.</u>) Recapture it, my arse. I should have known what would happen. Oh yes, there's the rub, frantically rushing round to switch off the fans. And I was the fool who engaged him. Oh yes, my wife has retained her attraction, as I know to my cost, particularly as <u>he</u> is only being treated to the more amiable aspects of Enid's character. And, of course, his attraction is not difficult to see, particularly when the heat of the mid-day sun requires him to walk around in nothing but tight bum-clinging little shorts, displaying a becomingly hairy chest and firm muscular thigh.

<u>Pause.</u>

He has 'comforted' her. Or if he hasn't yet, no doubt he soon will. (<u>Calls :</u>) Stay out there, Tim, there's nothing you can do. (Pause) Over the years husbands and wives learn the cruellest ways to humiliate each o0ther and this evening she has excelled herself. How I wish I could find consolation in indifference. Instead – (He drinks.) This speech you will not have learned by heart, it has not been prescribed for your examinations and you do not need to bombard me afterwards with boring interminable questions. You do not need to know what you think about it. You have only to listen. Be thankful for that.

He launches into a speech from **Othello**.

> Look here, Iago.
> All my fond love thus do I blow to heaven – 'tis gone.
> Arise, black vengeance, from the hollow hell!
> Yield up, O love, thy crown and hearted throne
> To tyrannous hate! Swell, bosom, with thy freight,
> For 'tis of aspics' tongues. …
> Like to the Pontic Sea,
> Whose icy current and compulsive course
> Ne'er knows retiring ebb, but keeps due on
> To the Propontic and the Hellespont,
> Even so my bloody thoughts with violent pace
> Shall ne'er look back, ne'er ebb to humble love,
> Till that a capable and wide revenge
> Swallow them up.

By the end he has tears in his eyes.

The whirligigs of time have their revenges. Why am I here? I asked to come. We said we wanted to do this tour and the answer came back: Oh, you can't just turn up and do what you like, oh no. We must find out what they want. And when because we wanted so desperately to come, we said we would do what they wanted, we were ever so graciously allowed to come. To this. To this. My grandfather would laugh in my face if he could see the state to which we are reduced.

Pause. He mops himself up.

I stand here before you in this hut. The generator whirs. The insects hum. You stare at me understandably puzzled, unbelievably polite. What can you make of me, of what I am? And what have I to say to you? I am here on sufferance because I still have a little knowledge you would like to possess. If it weren't for the Bard though, who today would listen to the words of an Englishman?

Pause. He pulls himself together.

I must apologise – for this disgraceful display. I shall carry with me from this trip one very real, very vivid memory. Of a scene that I saw two weeks ago in one of the smaller squares of your capital. A crowd was gathered, sitting in a circle, round something I couldn't at first see. It was a very mixed crowd of people, young and old, smartly dressed and shabby, babies and grandmothers, and they were laughing and cheering and even weeping. So I went closer. And there in a space specially cleared in the middle of the circle was a little old man, wizened and rather shabbily dressed. And he was telling the crowd stories, acting them out with voices and gestures. Just an old man without any props or costumes or even music but you could tell he was superb and the audience's attention was total. Enid laughed at the quaintness of the spectacle and I hated her. Because in some way, sentimental no doubt, unrealistic certainly, I wanted to be that old man.

Pause. He recites quietly:

Farewell, a long farewell, to all my greatness!
This is the state of man. Today he puts forth
The tender leaves of hopes; tomorrow blossoms,
And bears his blushing honours thick upon him;
The third day comes a frost, a killing frost…
And then he falls, as I do.

<u>Pause.</u>

I must conclude. Our tour will continue, as will your lives. The next time an English actor bearing Shakespeare comes this way, if he ever comes this way, he will probably come without a wife, without a Land Rover, without a stage manager, perhaps without anyone but himself. And I think it most likely he will never come at all.

<u>Pause.</u>

Thank you and good night.

<u>He leaves.</u>
<u>END</u>

THE LIMO FROM HELL

Written for David Gant

(**ONE**: Afternoon. DESMOND, smart casual up to date clothes, sits on a fashionably uncomfortable chair. He adjusts his clothing as if confronting an invisible video camera, clears his throat then triggers a remote control.

We live in extraordinary times. At least I do. Early this morning the doorbell rang and there was a man in a grey chauffeur's uniform. He ushered me into a beautiful matching grey Daimler and we glided off. I sat there in a dream all the way to Heathrow. But after all why should I be surprised? I am, after all, the face of today. Wizards, you see. Harry Potter, Gandalf, Merlin. Wizards are of now. Hunks have had their day. Wizards are the happening thing. Age before beauty. Maguses not muscle. In fact, I am so much the face of today that I may also be the face of tomorrow as well. And - since I'll be positively enhanced by wear and tear - I'm a face for today with a definite future.

(Pause)

If you listen to enough talk like this, you must end up going mad. Hence the video. Believe me, we will laugh about all this in years to come.

(Pause)

Of course, as you know, I didn't become the face of today overnight. I've waited fifty-nine years to be the face of today and I might have waited forever if we hadn't decided to buy table napkins in John Lewis. Personally, I'd have chucked the card away. The person who pressed it into my hand looked about three, their conversation made no sense and my mind was on table linen. You fished the card out of the bin, Luke. So you have to take the blame.

(Pause)

Anyway, here I am, the face of now, delivered safe and sound to a hotel in Cannes. And tomorrow I am a wizard selling life insurance. Well, in fact I'm a wizard trying to hold the tide back who should have had life insurance because his magic isn't working any more. Who just happens to be on a beach near Cannes. Something, I suppose, to do with the light. Or the type of sand. Or the fact that it's much nicer for the eminent photographer than a shoot on a beach near Bognor. Who am I to ask questions?

(Pause)

Let's face it, if I ask questions, they might find me out.

CUT TO –
(**TWO**: Evening. A more relaxed DESMOND.)

Mickey Baby asked me what music I liked to listen to. I thought a while and said – funky jazz, if you have any. And, of course, they had. So Thelonius Monk played and I stood on the sand wafting my six-foot wand while he snapped away. Mickey Baby that is, not Thelonius Monk. Perhaps it's not polite to call them snaps. After all, Mickey Baby is very famous. He's screwed more beautiful and famous women than seems humanly probable. I expected him to be a complete egomaniacal nightmare. But I liked him. There was no nonsense. He knew what he wanted and got on with it. It was only when the sea soaked his espadrilles that he got a bit tetchy. Who can blame him?

(Pause)

Over the grilled sardines at lunch, Mickey Baby said, "So have you always been a model, Deck?" And I wondered for a moment who he was talking to. Then I remembered that I was Deck. I blame the agency. They didn't fancy marketing a happening wizard called Desmond. Particularly a

Desmond who used to manage a gents' outfitters before early retirement loomed. Even one who's done the odd am-dram production of Agatha Christie. So I am Deck. No surname. Just Deck - as in chair. Mystery is now my business. I no longer give a straight answer to any question. So I'm afraid you have not featured in my conversation, Luke. Sexuality is not the issue. But being a minicab driver is. Deck does not know mini cab drivers, let alone live with them. Deck is enigmatic. Deck is aloof. And, Luke, I must be careful because Deck is, potentially, a pain in the arse.

(Pause)

Shall I tell you why I really liked old Mickey Baby? Of course, I've already earned my spurs. Proved to the madmen at the agency that chose me that they have not made a terrible mistake. I do not hide my face. I do not burst into nervous laughter. I do not blink at all the wrong moments – or demand to see the Polaroids and say, "Christ, I look awful. Can't you do something about my nose?" I have delivered the goods. But this is different. This is big. This is the real thing. So - we'd been working all day and before the light went, he said, "This is your moment." "I'm sorry," I said. "This is your moment," he repeated. "I've got all I need. There's film in the camera and half an hour left. Just do what you want."

(Pause. DESMOND rises.)

So I got up – and I thought, "Thelonius Monk is playing. What the hell?" And I looked out to sea and forgot the camera. I raised my hands and greeted the sea. Big sweeping gestures. Then I knelt on the sand, bugger the trousers. And I worshipped the sea, head down on the sand, hands clasped. And then I lay on the sand, feet towards the sea, arms outstretched like Jesus and forgot everything in the sheer beauty of my surroundings.

(Pause. The gestures cease. He stands there, very still. Finally he speaks:)

I know, I just know, that the final photo he will use for this ad is somewhere in that last thirty minutes. Don't ask me how. I just know.

(Pause)

I've never experienced anything like it. OK, the camera was clicking away all the time but I didn't care. I was in control. I knew what to do. I was in the moment. I was of the moment. I've never had a buzz like it.

(He stands quiet and still. A long pause. Then :)

Don't worry, Luke. I haven't forgotten you.

CUT TO:
(**THREE**: Afternoon. DESMOND, seated again, animated, more confident with the video equipment)

The driver was late but I decided not to make a fuss. The traffic was probably shitty and after all it was only five minutes. Well, six minutes, now I come to think of it but we still made the plane. I remember the cautionary tale, Luke. An extremely famous prima donna in a chauffeur-driven limo. She rings her agent to ring the car hire company to ring the driver to tell him to drive slower. That way madness lies.

(Pause)

You'd adore this place, Luke. Scottish baronial. Log fires crackling. Aged retainers with whisky bottles. Dead deer mounted on the wall. Delightful company. Delicious food. What an extraordinary way to make lots of money. The only snag is that we have to be up so bloody early, none of us can afford to eat or drink very much.

(Pause)

I am an abbot – with lines. "Ah, yes," as – attended by a young acolyte - I open a rare cask in the vaults of my ancient abbey. "Ah, yes, yes," as I smell the contents. And "Ah, yes, yes, yes," as I sample a drop. My final line is a profound sigh of pleasure. The agency suggested four yeses but the clients wanted the sigh instead. It befits the old-world image of the product apparently. Not, as you might think, a wine but a brand of antiseptic mouthwash. I'm going to have a word rehearsal before I go to bed. I'm up at six. My first big film commercial.

(Pause. He practises :)

Ah, yes. Ah, yes, yes. Ah, yes, yes, yes. Aaaah.

CUT TO:
(**FOUR**: Evening. DESMOND relaxed)

First day's shoot went well. Even the though the ruined abbey was freezing. Thirty seconds in ten hours which, I gather, is going it some. The director seemed pleased. And I was pleased too because the four yeses went back in. After much to-ing and fro-ing with the clients and a three way phone conversation between Scotland, Los Angeles and Madrid. So "Ah, yes, yes, yes, yes!!!" it was. A tribute, I think, to the intensity I was bringing to the six yeses before. Deck was delivering the goods.

(Pause)

Sat next to my co-star at supper, Darren. He plays the acolyte. Well, I called him my co-star to be polite but he's really only support. If Darren's anything to go by, the monks in my abbey are all gym bunnies. Square jaw, blue eyes, blond curly hair, not a lot going on up top. Nice boy but not my type. No chemistry there – even if we didn't have to get up and do the refectory sequence tomorrow. No temptation. None. Not at all. Ah, no, no, no, no.

(Pause)

Darren said he loved the wizard on the sands. There was a big buzz in the agency about it. Well, it's true. The image seems to have got everywhere. Newspapers, magazines, billboards. I explained that the pose had been my idea and he was impressed. He's not bright enough to come up with something like that. Of course, I insisted that credit was still due to the photographer. I don't want to take away from what he brought. But – put it this way, I said - I more than earned my money.

(Pause)

We discussed 'the buzz'. He gets it too. Better than sex, he said. Even better than coke, which clearly was a <u>big</u> tribute. But photo-shoots were all about you. Filming involved others. It wasn't the same. But he said – if you want the buzz to end all buzzes – try the catwalk.

CUT TO:
(**FIVE**: Night. DESMOND, very wired, speaking very fast.)

You should have been here, Luke. I can't believe you missed it. It's been extraordinary, out of this world. And I can't believe that I ever thought it was bound to fall apart. Because it didn't, it really didn't. It was fantastic. I mean you're in the middle of the town square somewhere in Italy and there are all these marquees but they haven't been put up yet and there's all this seating but that hasn't been put up either. And you think – madness. I give up. I want to go home. It's two now, at eight there's a show. It won't happen. It can't. But then something happens. You go into this marquee they haven't finished putting up and there's this skinny guy and he's say, "Hi, I'm Mauro" and he's my dresser. And there, miracle of miracles, are all the clothes I'm to wear up there on my personal hanger and for an even bigger miracle they all fit. Well, actually the jackets all fit, the trousers are a bit of a disaster, so there's pinning and tucking and clipping. But you look around you and everywhere there's pinning and tucking and clipping. And suddenly you feel the whole world is being staple gunned to stop it falling down. So then, nipped and tucked, suited and sutured, you try on the shoes, great flashy designer shoes, and they're too big. Two sizes too big. So we're stuffing socks and tissue paper and God knows what into them and I clump over to the stage for the rehearsal. And there it is – the catwalk. Except it's not finished. So this crazy woman with blue hair and staring eyes emerges and greets me and the rest of the guys and this is Simona, the choreographer. So she takes us through our moves. Suddenly she screams: "Deck, now you!!!" So I come on, trying not to fall off the edge and I do my twirls and turns. (He demonstrates) Then I walk back, with Simona clapping hands to keep the rhythm as the guy who's just coming on nearly bumps into me. This goes on for hours. My trousers nearly fall down but Mauro pins them up. I miss an entrance and Simona screams, "Deck! Deck! Where is

Deck?" and I would have replied if I'd had any clothes on at the time. And because of the shoes it's like I'm on a skiing holiday. And then – suddenly – the rehearsals are over and it's thank you very much, good luck for tonight. And then you notice this podgy guy dressed in black – they're always dressed in black – who's been watching and he looks sick with nerves and is having a tantrum over some jacket or other and fifteen assistants scurry round him. And then you think – it's time I went and chilled out with Sergio. Because you think - the trousers are going to fall down, the shoes are going to fly off, the catwalk's going to collapse and you'll miss an entry and then rush on and realise you're wearing nothing but your underpants. So you think – keep upbeat – and you stuff yourself full of chocolate biscuits and yoghurt and crisps and whatever else is on offer from Sergio because that's what everybody else is doing. Bugger diets, bugger gyms, bugger waistlines, what we need is comfort food and energy, energy, energy. Then before you know it, there are calls and you're being helped into your opening outfit. I have five outfits – three minutes between each change. It's possible, Mauro assures me. In fact he says it time and time again. It's bedlam backstage, more pins, more tucks, more clips. The air so heady with hair spray you could pass out. Finally, it's your turn to crouch just out of sight in this cramped little entrance booth beside a stage manager on headphones who's a midget. She has to be, nobody else could fit in the available space. And behind you, it's still chaos. And beyond is God knows what. And suddenly the midget taps you and you're on. You pull back the flap. Very deliberately you pick up on the rhythm of the model who's just come off and you emerge from the chaos into the music and the lights and the crowd.

(DESMOND takes the stage as on a catwalk)

All those eyes upon you. There's nothing quite like it. Applause for your outfit. You walk slowly and lightly as if you owned the whole world. Applause for your walk. You love all those people out there and they love you. They love your hair, the way you walk, the clothes you wear. You are a star. You acknowledge your public. And at the end of the catwalk, you turn with a flourish and you float back. And as you leave, there's more applause. Well, there was for me. Sergio said I'd got it wrong – it was for the model just coming in. But I <u>knew</u> it was mine. The next model wasn't in sight. Four times it happened. Four times. Every time – the buzz, the love, the applause. Finally the designer came on and we all came on with him. And he doesn't look podgy and ill, he looks happy and proud. And we're all happy and proud and we applaud him and he applauds us and the audience applauds us all and it just goes on and on. The audience wanted me to take a solo bow - I could tell. But the other models weren't having any of it. They were jealous. They kept pushing me back. But the audience loved me all the same. I just know they did. I could feel it. It was fantastic. Oh, there's not a high like it. I want to do it all over again. Well, maybe with better shoes. No, fuck, it was great, just great. Just great.

CUT TO:
(**SIX:** Later. DESMOND, subdued, seated, tense)

You should have been here, Luke. What went wrong? Why didn't you come? Did you miss the plane – or what?

(Pause)

I've been down in the bar with Sergio. Sergio as in "try some of this." He tried to tell me I'd fucked up. They were pissed off with me. But he was wrong. I didn't fuck up, Luke. I was great. You really should have seen it. <u>Pause)</u> You really should have seen it.

CUT TO:
(**SEVEN:** DESMOND, expansive and tetchy - but very matter-of-fact now with the video controls)

Well, the limo was late this time – seven minutes late. What am I supposed to do? This is an important contract and I don't expect to twiddle my thumbs. And as for the limo – I couldn't believe my eyes. It was filthy. There were traces of cigarette ash in the ashtrays. And smears over the back window. And the chauffeur hadn't brushed his shoes in days. And as I got out, I noticed a scratch on the left front bumper. I pointed to it. He claimed not to see it. I'm making a complaint. Just my luck – I'm going on a highly important assignment – on which I might add a great deal depends – and they send me the limo from hell.

(Pause)

Anyway, here I am – after a pretty bloody flight – in Morocco. Marrakesh. The air condition is making a dreadful noise and the complimentary soap leaves a lot to be desired but at least I'm here. Hurrah!

(Pause)

I was greeted with the information that they'd made reservations for us at three different restaurants. Would I look to choose which one we'd all like? I mean, for God's sake! Can't they make a decision? Don't I have enough on my plate without having to choose a bloody restaurant? I am the wicked wazir. I am at the centre of probably the most important promotion of fitted carpets Europe will see this year. For God's sake!!!

CUT TO:
(**EIGHT**: Night. DESMOND quiet and depressed.)

Well, here I am back at the hotel. He's just left. The boy, that is. There was a bit of difficulty getting him past reception but a few extra dirhams did the trick. I mean, he wasn't a boy boy. In Moroccan terms he's probably getting on. But he suited me. He was cute. Lovely eyes. Black curly hair. And very accommodating.

(Pause)

After it was over, he even tried to make conversation. He asked me why I was there in Marrakesh and I tried to explain. I stand in front of the camera. People take photos of me. They dress me up. They ask me to do things. I know it sounds easy, I said, but there are always people out there willing you to fail. Kif just wouldn't do the business. I even demonstrated the sort of things I was expected to do. There was a grave pause. His lovely eyes stared at me puzzled. He couldn't believe it. Well, I suppose, he has a point. He must work pretty hard for his money too sometimes.

(Pause)

Frankly, it's been bloody today. In the circumstances I've got a pretty good deal. The agency stood by me. After the usual three way conversations to Los Angeles, Chipping Sudbury and Tel Aviv, I'm getting the full fee and all expenses. It's a drag I won't get the residuals but c'est la vie.

(Pause)

If you're dealing with a pack of arseholes like this, there's only so much you can take. I can't be expected to create my magic when they're being so bloody picky. They accused me of being high on set. I bloody well wasn't. Anyone could see. And then they told me I was fidgeting on camera. I went ballistic. I do not fidget on camera. Hadn't they seen the wizard on the sands? I created that image. If they want a fucking wazir to sell their crap carpets then I'm their man. Wazirs and wizards are what I do. I'm the face of now.

(Pause)

When I said that, somebody laughed. It was the last straw.

CUT TO:
(**NINE:** Morning. Time has passed. DESMOND is quiet and withdrawn)

Here I am still talking to you. It's got to be a habit. Maybe one day you'll catch up on all this.

(Pause)

There's no place like home I don't bloody think. It's grim. I miss you. I miss the cat. And I miss the phone going. To be perfectly frank, it's not been going very often recently.

(Pause)

Shall I tell you something funny? At least I think it's funny. I'm not always sure what to laugh at these days. Well, the agency does try. They do put me up for jobs. And I went to see these people about a soft drinks commercial. I was going to be an elderly conjurer at a kiddies' party. Well, when I got there, there was a roomful of men my sort of age and build sitting there. Some of them I knew to say hello to but nobody made eye contact. People read newspapers or books or stared at the floor. Every now and then somebody would be summoned. But nobody looked up when a name was called. It was like being in a V.D. clinic.

(Pause)

Well, finally, it was me who was summoned. A bored American who didn't even say hello. The assistant showed me a clipping from a magazine. "We're looking for someone like this," she said. I stared. It was a picture of me, the picture of me. The wizard in the sand, the photo I made happen. So I said, "But this is extraordinary. This is a picture of me." The assistant smiled politely. The boss didn't even look up. He gestured impatiently towards a waiting camera. There was a closed circuit tie-up to the clients in New York. "Just say your name and agency, Deck," the fat American growled. So I did. And then I said my line. "Ho, ho, ho," I said. "Ho, ho, ho…"

(Pause)

Of course they didn't give me the job. That's what's funny, Luke. These days I can't even get a job as me.

Slow fade.)

THE END

TINKLING THE IVORIES

Elise was played by Dora Bryan
Radio 4.
2006

Directed by Martin Jenkins

For Pier Productions, Brighton

<u>A piano plays romantic film music.
Then over this, ELISE's voice.</u>

I shall always remember that first time. I was only fourteen and very very nervous. My knees were shaking and my hands were clammy and clamped to the side of my best dress. Somehow I made it to the organ and somehow I sat down and I unclamped my clammy hands and I started to play. After that, everything was perfect. Well, when it came to playing music anyway.

<u>Pause.</u>

People often ask me 'where does all that music come from?' Truth is I don't really know. But it was always there inside me waiting to come out. When mum and dad were screaming at each other and my brothers and sisters were squabbling, I'd just close my eyes and there it was. Like my name. You see, I was christened Elsie but I always knew deep down that I was really called Elise. So as soon as the opportunity came along I called myself Elise. Then I became Elise Fortunata. Queen of the Keyboards. Empress of the Organ. It was easy enough to do because inside that's who I'd always been.

<u>Pause.</u>

But I do owe a debt to my Auntie Gertie. She was my mother's older sister and she'd married Uncle Harold who was very well off but they never had any children. Don't know why - mother said it was because Uncle Harold wasn't a proper man. But I didn't care because I was Auntie Gertie's favourite.

<u>Pause.</u>

Uncle Harold had inherited an old upright. It was a terrible old thing really. The soft pedal had dropped off and the felt had gone on most of the dampers so it sounded more like a ukulele than a piano. But one day I sat down and started playing a tune. Something I'd heard on the radio. Tea for Two. You know, "Picture you upon my knee, just tea for two and two for tea…"

(She stops.)

I can still see her face - Auntie Gertie - standing there - staring. She thought it was extraordinary. Whereas it seemed perfectly natural to me. She told my mother I should have lessons. And she paid for them so mum could hardly object. Miss Baxter was a nasty old tyrant - used to slap my wrists with a ruler when I went wrong. But she couldn't stop me enjoying what I did. And then Auntie Gertie told our local fleapit about my talents.

(Pause.)

Those black and white images are still as fresh today as when I first saw them. My eyes would see and my hands would play. It was seamless. I wasn't thinking, just feeling – everything was so rich, so romantic, so exciting, so mysterious.

(Pause.)

Flesh and the Devil. That was a favourite. Everybody remembers Greta Garbo vamping all these men, and, of course, I'd be the first to admit she was wonderful. But it was John Gilbert for me. So handsome. So manly. All that dark hair and that lovely moustache. Whispering silent words of passion for which I found the music.

(Pause.)

Poor John Gilbert. When sound came, he just sounded daft saying all those 'sweet nothings'. Much better when my music played and the members of audience imagined what he was saying. I still carried a bit of a candle for him though. Even when I just played in the interval and he was left spouting these silly words in his slightly squeaky voice – wasn't quite so manly then. I'd married my first husband because he looked a bit like John Gilbert. That was a big mistake.

(Pause.)

Of course, I don't want to give the impression that doing what I do is easy. I knew from an early age that not everybody could do what I did and I had to know all styles and all sorts of music - Grand opera - .Light operetta - Light classics – 0h and 'Contemporary' – which when I started meant anything from Bix Beiderdecke to Bye Bye Blackbird. Bye Bye Blackbird was my first husband's favourite song. It's the one melody out of the thousands in my head I wish I'd forgotten.

(Pause.)

I never had a problem finding the right music to fit each appropriate moment - that was easy - the problem was not knowing what was going to happen next. You'd never seen the film before so how could you? Sometimes you'd look up and see cars chasing across the screen so that would be fast jazzy chase music. Then suddenly the audience would get restless - well, that's putting it mildly – they'd start booing on occasion, even bombard me with tomatoes. Because there you were still imagining a chase and up on the screen two lovers were canoodling in a moonlit garden.

(Pause.)

It was quite simple really. My first husband thought my parents were vulgar losers - my parents thought he was a pretentious drunk who would hit me about. Unfortunately for me they were both right. Thank God I never had any children.

(Pause.)

I didn't know when I started that I was 'the end of an era' .Sound simply took over – out went the cinema orchestras and then even little organs like mine. We weren't wanted – films came with voices and music already attached. And that was that.

(Pause.)

I think it was a terrible shame. The immediacy was gone. When I playing and watching the film along with the audience, I was feeling what they were feeling. I was happy when they were happy, sad when they were sad. The cinema may have been an old fleapit but we weren't just watching, we were imagining, we were participating. But who was I to swim against the tide? I was just a snotty young girl.

(She breaks into song :)

"Oh I do like to be beside the seaside, beside the seaside, beside the sea..." That was his name - Reginald - my first husband that is – like Reginald Dixon. If he was in a bad mood, he'd thump me. But he knew an opportunity when he saw it. Silent films were gone. Cinema managers weren't going to fork out large sums of money for someone to play in the interval when all anyone wanted was iced cream. But organs were getting bigger and better. As my first husband often used to say. He could be a mucky bastard when he wanted for all his supposed refinement. But he was right.

(Pause.)

So there I was – beside the seaside – playing the mighty Wurlitzer – well, a small version of it - in some of the smartest ballrooms on the South Coast. Mind you, it was all 'dirty weekends' stuff. That's what they were there for, most of them. As one of the slogans said: "The Tivoli Hotel where you can feel a good friend…" It was Reginald's idea of seventh heaven. While I was playing the organ, he was – well, I don't need to say it, do I?

(Pause.)

I wanted the music to stay romantic but it doesn't, does it? John Gilbert didn't last so why should my marriage? Reginald went off with some floozy – taking our savings - and by the time I saw him in the divorce court most of it was gone. The next night I was playing the Arrival of the Queen of Sheba for a ballroom full of people who'd registered in as 'Mr and Mrs Smith'. Or perhaps 'Mr and Mrs Brown' if they were feeling more creative.

(Pause.)

The bruises, literal and metaphorical, faded. I played on. I was good too. Always ready for the special requests. (Concerned voice :) 'The Man I Love', darling? Of course. One of my favourites too. I've only played it four times this week so far." Always immaculately attired. Well, if the films weren't there to sparkle, you had to do a bit of sparkling on your own account, didn't you? But most of the time I was playing with my eyes closed. Imagining how things might be. Remembering how things used to be.

(Pause.)

I had a good war. People used to say to me, "You mustn't say that, Elise." But I'm so old now that I don't have to bother – I can say what I like. And I did have a good war. It changed my life. When the men went off to fight, the women moved up a notch and I got to play bigger and better organs. Oh, I can just imagine Reginald sniggering at that. But it wasn't the instruments that made the difference, it was the atmosphere. People were snatching pleasure where they could - while they could. When you played you were responding to all that energy, all that hope, all that fear, all that heartbreak and all that love. Any moment a bomb might drop - wipe it all away. Suddenly I didn't want to close my eyes any more. One day I opened them and saw Michael – god bless him.

(Pause.)

Oh he wasn't a bit like John Gilbert. Or Cary Grant. Or Clark Gable. More like Stanley Holloway really - lovely warm friendly eyes - funny sweet sticky-out ears. And do you know - he thought I was the most glamorous thing he'd ever seen. Or so he said. And who was I to contradict him? He knew he couldn't ask me to dance so he waited for me at the stage door. Of course, he wasn't the first man who'd done that. . Men are hornier than ever in wartime and a lady in a sequinned top and a few sparklers tinkling away at the ivories will always arouse attention. Usually it was more arousal than attention - but with Michael – well – he was different. He was on leave, you see - didn't rush anything - a proper gentleman.

(Pause.)

He really loved me. How did I know? I just did. I didn't need to think about it. And I loved him.

(Pause.)

It was strange though. He took me to a matinee of 'Gone with the Wind'. And when I heard Max Steiner's wonderful music, it was the first time, the first time ever, I hadn't thought 'that ought to be me playing' It was a habit I'd got into, you see - listening to the music in my head instead of the music out there accompanying the film. But this time I really heard and felt Steiner's music, every last chord of it. Michael held my hand and I cried, oh how I cried.

(Pause.)

At the end of the war back Michael came home safe and sound - still looked the same - still loved me and I still loved him. We bought this pub - he served beer and I played the piano. Oh, I'd play anything. I moved with the times – rocked with the best - Bill Hayley and his Comets. Elvis Presley. The Beatles. Diana Ross and the Supremes – all that hair and 'baby love' – but now it was easy you see - I wasn't that anxious little girl any more - in love with my heroes of the silver screen. I had Michael - I had the pub and all our friends and…

(Pause.)

He was like Clark Gable in one way though – Michael - when he – well - when he died of his heart attack – he was barely sixty too. What was I to do? I sold up – had just about enough to live on - but I was dead inside - suddenly there was no music – anywhere!

(Pause.)

I wasn't young. But I wasn't old. Not old old. And there were gentlemen because there are always gentlemen who were interested. It's all about organs, I can hear Reginald sniggering. Anyway, I just sat there in this bungalow by the sea and waited - for what? For death, I suppose. But it didn't come. So after a time you start to get bored.

(Pause.)

Don't know how they found me. But they did. Phone rang. 'Miss Elise Fortunata? – a prestigious season of silent classics' they said. 'We believe you used to be an accompanist before sound came along'. 'Yes', I said, 'I am several centuries old'. Then I said to myself, "Elise, don't be horrible. These are nice well-meaning young men and they love the things you used to love." So I said yes.

(Pause.)

And there I was back in touch with the gods and goddesses of my childhood. And - suddenly there it was - FLESH AND THE DEVIL – all spruced up – just as it had never been out of my life – there they were John Gilbert and Greta Garbo touching cigarettes in the dark So romantic and sexy too, if we're using modern terms. It was done with little batteries in the cigarette ends but who cares? And John Gilbert was still there just as he always was. And when I played, I knew what he was saying and how much better it was than the awful dialogue they gave him afterwards. And all the young people were very polite and thought it was amazing that I could still do it. I shocked them all once at the National Film Theatre. I was accompanying this film made in 1928 sixty years later and at the end I turned to the audience and said – "It's just as good as when I saw it first " Well, that made them think.

(Pause.)

So my real life ended where it began. Looking up at the screen and tinkling the ivories. There are worse ways to end up. It's a tribute to that determined little girl who went up to Auntie Gertie's upright and played Tea for Two.

(Pause.)

Only one question now I'd like the answer to. What it's going to sound like? Death, I mean. Will it be harps? And trumpets? Something lovely soft, warm and welcoming? That's what I always tried to convey anyway. But who knows what it will really be like when you go. That's where imagination comes in – too many people don't really think anymore ……………..

(Silence. Then a deep sigh.)

I'm hearing the most heavenly music now. Are you?

(Silence)
END

THE ICEMAN RETURNETH

Written for Paul Scofield

Commissioned by Pier Productions.

(The sounds of a mountain blizzard.)
(As it subsides, the Ice Man speaks :)

I had been lying in frozen peace for five thousand years. Or it could be four and a half thousand years. Or perhaps five and a half thousand years. It's difficult to tell when you're completely trapped in ice. Time doesn't just go slowly. Time doesn't go at all.

(Pause.)

Then from somewhere came a feeling of slight warmth. Very slight at first but gradually more and more - then gradually again some moisture creeping around my shrivelled leathery body. Gradually, of course, could mean a hundred years or ten days or perhaps ten minutes, how do I know? But the fact was that the ice around me was beginning to thaw. I was emerging from my icy coffin and being returned to the outside world. Time started to move – for others if not for me.

(Pause.)

I knew that someday somebody would surely find me. Of course, how long I would have to wait I couldn't tell. Years, months, days, minutes. What did it matter? Finally there were footsteps – footsteps across the ice – and they stopped. Two voices – a man voice and a woman voice, neither of them sounding young. They talked in whispers even though they were alone on top of a glacier. They sounded shocked and even frightened. There was an argument, still in hushed tones. The only words I heard clearly were words that held no meaning for me. The man voice said "Shall I take a photograph?" and the woman voice replied "Don't. It's not respectful to the dead." And the man said, "If that was someone I knew, I'd want to show how they died." The woman argued but in the end

The Man Who Found Me said, "There's one shot left. I'm taking it."

(Pause.)

They left - there was silence again - but I knew that this time it would not be infinite silence. Soon there were more footsteps across the ice. And then thwack! blows showering down on the ice around me. I had always thought I would like to be freed from eternal frozen constraint. But now I was not so sure. I sensed eyes upon me. Lights flashed. The axes hacked. And soon I was exposed to the new world. Naked, vulnerable, a shrivelled shadow of what I once was. No clothes, no weapons, no defence. I knew that my clothes lay shattered and shredded in the ice around. Somewhere was my bow and arrow. Somewhere my axe. Somewhere my small supply of food. Of course, I couldn't tell them that. But then I'm not sure I would have wanted to. Mystery was all I had to protect me.

(Pause.)

They carried me away from the mountain top - my home for so many thousands of years. They carried me from one strange place to another strange place and – unless I am mistaken – carried me back and repeated this again and again. Sometimes I was re-frozen. Sometimes my body was covered in strange ointments. If my sightless eyeballs had been able to see there would have been extraordinary sights to be seen.

(Pause.)

There was one voice which I think of as belonging to The Chief Among Men – a determined voice, not always the loudest, not always the most talkative, but at the end when the other voices trailed away, it was his which was heard. The Chief Among Men made an important speech about 'The Ice Man' - that was what they called me – the Ice

Man. Well, you can see there was logic even if no great imagination.

(Pause.)

The Chief Among Men told them that finding me was a miracle – never before had the perfectly preserved body of a five thousand year old man been discovered. I had been caught in a blizzard. I had sheltered behind a rock. I had become exhausted. I had frozen to death. Who was I to know whether they were right or not?

(Pause.)

Then The Chief Among Men unfolded great plans for what must be done. Some of them would take tiny fragments of my flesh and study them. Others would put me inside strange metal machines and ponder my brain. Others would scrape my stomach to find what food I ate. Others would discover the meaning of the tattoos upon my body. Others would look at the fragments of clothing still attached to my skin. Others would look at why my genitals appeared to have disappeared.

(Pause.)

Ah yes, my genitals. Well, all in good time.

(Pause.)

The Man Who Found Me visited me. He was the only one who actually talked to me. I liked that. He told me he and his woman were fifty years old. He worked in something called a public library and she worked in personnel. What the terms meant I had no idea but I liked the way he confided in me. "We have no children," he said, "so we like to spend our holidays hiking in the mountains." Holidays? Hiking? But the flow of his warm, friendly voice soothed me and in so far as a mummified five thousand year old corpse can feel affection I felt it for him. Perhaps something told me I once had a family I loved.

(Pause.)

"You are the most exciting thing that had ever happened to me in my whole life," he continued. "You have given my life meaning. I am very proud of what I've given the world." Then he told me that he was being called my father by other people because he was the one who had found me. But he said "I don't think I am your father. I think of you as my brother. Maybe because I've never had a brother. Maybe" – but he stopped at that point because I think he was worried that he'd said something rather strange.

(Pause.)

Then he told me something else. And I could tell he was a bit ashamed. It was about the photograph his woman had told him not to take. At first he had been so proud of finding me that he'd given copies to anyone who asked for one. But then somebody had told his woman that they shouldn't be giving them away for nothing. People would give money for them. There was money to be made out of me. "We argued over it but then we thought – why not? Didn't we find him and given him to the world? Why shouldn't we be rewarded?" But his voice didn't sound happy when he said that.

(Pause.)

Then suddenly there was a new Chief Among Men. Another confident warrior He too went on talking after everyone else stopped. The first Chief Among Men had been a fool and a charlatan – or that's what the new one said to his assistants when he was with me behind closed doors. The theory of how I died was wrong. I didn't freeze to death stranded in a blizzard. He'd come up with a much better explanation. There had been a massacre in my village. Enemies had descended and slaughtered men, women and children. I had escaped but at a cost. My equipment was badly damaged and I was wounded. So I died bleeding and exhausted from the struggle to evade my pursuing enemies. Well, it was certainly more dramatic.

(Pause.)

But this second Chief Among Men was not believed by everyone. There was a rumour that I was a fake – a mummy from an Egyptian tomb dropped in ice and dragged to the surface again. The proof? I had no genitals which meant I had to come from a society where dead bodies were castrated. So the search was on. Well, if you must know, one day a woman reached down and pulled them out. Somehow they'd been overlooked in previous examinations. Do not demand of me how that is possible. I had always known they were down there - somewhere.

(Pause.)

So this new Chief Among Men triumphed and I stopped being moved from place to place. Although there was not a day when somebody didn't come to probe or examine. Apparently they knew more about me than I did - not only how I died but what I ate and what I wore and why I had tattoos and what my face looked like. After a great struggle they'd even worked out what my shoes were like.

(Pause.)

The Man Who Found Me came to see me. He was upset, somehow different from the time before. Not to me. I was still his brother. But because I was his brother, he believed I would understand. I did my best. He said to me – "Selling the photographs set me and my wife thinking. There's money being made from you, Ice Man, and there are experts getting grants and publishing books and building careers and going on television – so what about me? The

Man Who Found You? The man who understood you? I've got nothing. The money they've spent on you would have kept a thousand dying people alive. So I decided I was going to claim a reward for finding you. But it hasn't been easy. I've had to fight and fight. It wasn't that anybody has ever said no. It was that nobody has ever said yes. So I'm fighting on."

(Pause.)

All this had taken years of my life, he said. But what were years to me? I couldn't tell how many years I'd been in the ice. Now I couldn't tell how long I'd been out of it. But I knew his voice had changed. There was still the pride in finding me. But there was a bitterness, an anger, a sense that life had not dealt with him fairly. The others around me seethed with bitterness too – mostly against each other. But his was sadder, a man who'd been led to believe that he was important and then somehow been forgotten. "I love nature," he said, "and I love you, Ice Man. All I ask is for a plaque to be erected on the mountain near where we found you to record what my wife and I did." Except I don't think that would really have satisfied him. Nothing would now.

(Pause.)

Then there was another Chief Among Men. And another. And another. Sometimes two of them were in my presence together shouting at each other. Sometimes three. One day one of these men finally spoke to me directly. "I am sick of dealing with you," he shouted. "I'm sick of thinking about you. It's destroying everything, my marriage included. I hate you, Ice Man, and I wish you'd never come into my life." I would have like to have said that the feeling was mutual.

(Pause.)

But then they found an arrowhead buried in the left side of my chest. Arrowheads. Genitals. You'd think with all their much vaunted skills these were things they couldn't miss, wouldn't you? But then what do I know? I'm just a leathery old defrosted corpse.

(Pause.)

But now there could be a new theory. Everything that had been said before was wrong. I had been shot dead with an arrow. Oh this was much better - shot from below it ripped through my nerves and major blood vessels and shattered my left shoulder blade. I would have lived only a few hours after this untreated wound. Well, it's certainly even more dramatic. Sometimes I have wanted to suggest that maybe I was a ritual sacrifice served up upon the altar of some savage unknown god. But I suspect they'll get come round to that sooner or later.

(Pause.)

Tired. So tired. I feel myself moving away from all this. It is as if I am returning to the ice. Someone has found two fleas in the remaining fragments of my clothing. Someone has studied my teeth and worked out what sort of water I was drinking which in turn tells them where I came from. As the man who hated me said, this is never going to end. There will always be new tests. There will always be new techniques. It will never stop. A terrible lassitude pervades my bones. I long to be frozen again. I long not to know.

(Pause.)

The last thing perhaps that I will ever remember was a visit from the Man Who Found Me. His voice was harsh with bitterness. "I wish I had never found you. My wife is sick with worry and I can see no way forward. You've destroyed us."

(Pause.)

Then he continued - "People believe there is a curse on you, Ice Man. Do you know how many of the experts who've squabbled and fought over you have died? Sometimes they're killed in accidents. Sometimes their hearts give out unexpectedly. Sometimes they've got sick with cancers and withered away."

(Pause.)

And I thought of the man who had screamed at me and realised – they think they love me but they hate me. They know they will never find the truth. They know that their version of the truth will last the blinking of an eyelid. And yet they cannot walk away and leave me to others – or to myself. But the only one I pitied was the Man Who Found Me. He loved me. I gave his life meaning. And now he wished he'd never found me. He talked about hiking once more on the mountains where he'd found me. And I thought – they'll find him dead and frozen like me. Except that he won't get one thousandth of the attention.

(Pause.)

I withdraw more and more. I think of myself back in the ice. I think of myself knowing nothing. But something strange has happened. I had a picture in my head. A picture of something before I froze in ice. It's not clear. It's not vivid. But I think I am waving goodbye to my woman and to a boy and two girls on the day I started to climb the mountain. Goodbye, I call, Goodbye.

(The blizzard returns.)

END

HO! HO! HO!

Desmond was played by Bernard Cribbins.
Radio 4
Christmas 2007

Directed by Martin Jenkins

For Pier Productions

(Badly amplified Christmas muzak)
(Then, as this fades, Leonard's voice:)

Ho! Ho! Ho! (Pause) Ho! Ho! Ho! (Pause) Ho! Ho! Ho! Ho! (Pause) You try saying that five hundred times a day as if you meant it. Ho! Ho! Ho! Little girl! Ho! Ho! Ho! Little boy! Ho! Ho! Ho! Loud-mouthed group of half-pissed teenagers looking for trouble! Maybe I should have been content with my lot. It's not every man in his early seventies who has a Christmas job which pays him a few bob, gets him out of the house and gives him a chance to meet new people. But there comes a time when the "ho! ho! ho!"–ing has to stop. And this year it came.

(Pause.)

Well, I suppose you could start with the perpetual problem of the lousy amplification system. It's a huge shopping centre. All the shops in there are going to make a mint over Christmas. There are Christmas lights everywhere. Messages saying Happy Christmas, Seasons Greetings and Merry Xmas. Xmas, well, don't get me started on that. Then there are Christmas bunnies, Christmas fairies, Christmas angels, Christmas holly, Christmas snow – and I have to admit a very impressive Christmas tree under which I sit. If they hadn't buried it in baubles and glitter, it'd be a handsome sight. At least until the tree starts moulting and the pine needles drop down the back of my neck. So in their ghastly commercial way the people who run this place don't mind spending a few bob. So why not spend some money on a decent amplification system? Every year I ask. And this year I nearly had a stand-up row with the jobsworth called Kevin who manages the centre.

(Pause)

He couldn't see the problem. I said that it's so distorted and so loud you can't really tell whether it's playing "Oh Come

All Ye Faithful" or "Walking in a Winter Wonderland." He said I was being an old fogey. People today like their music that loud and it was in keeping with the overall upbeat ambience of the centre. So that was that as far as he was concerned.

(Pause.)

Actually I do know what the tunes are because there are only five of them and they go round and round and round in my head. Hearing Jinglebells approximately fifty a day must do things to the brain.

(Pause.)

Funny how all this Santa business started. Penny and I were on holiday in Turkey. It was a beautiful warm July evening and we were eating seafood on the beach. We were relaxed, tanned and happy. There was a sound system playing golden oldies and Penny started singing along. I joined in. And then suddenly there was a click and there was Bing Crosby singing "I'm Dreaming of a White Christmas." In July! In Turkey! We couldn't stop laughing. And then Penny said – "You know, Leonard, if you grew your beard a bit, you'd make a very good Father Christmas."

(Pause)

So I'd got this job as a Santa in a department store, nothing like as big as this. It was a bit of a lift after the enforced early retirement. And Penny and I share this silly sense of humour. So when we got our kitten, we called it Rudolph. Rudolph the red-nosed kitten. Even though he's a tabby. He was a good luck charm for my new job.

(Pause.)

Well, it all went well. I was good at the job and I actually enjoyed it back then. Although I soon discovered there are advantages and disadvantages to having your own beard for the job. No child is going to pull it off and burst into tears when they realise it's false. On the other hand it's agony while they try. I also came with my own paunch which spared me the padding. But after all these years, the centre management still expect me to wear a costume made of nylon. Sweating away under the lights, I sometimes thought I was generating enough static electricity to supply half of Manchester.

(Pause.)

And sitting there day after day, all sorts of things come into your mind. Is it just me or are children different these days? The real children I mean, not teenagers out of their heads on God knows what bunking off from school and ready to threaten Father Christmas with GBH. No, the ones who still believe in Santa. I'm a bit of a softy really. Innocent young faces wishing and hoping for something special. Our Sally was like that as a kid. She didn't expect the earth.

(Pause.)

When I started this job, you still used to ask a kid what they thought Santa was going to bring them and there was a maybe he will, maybe he won't feel about it. Not these days. Nowadays they want everything. And they expect everything too. They reel off bloody shopping lists – x pods, z pods, gameboys, playstations, MP3s, MP4s, whatever they all are, I just nod. And not just any x y or z pods, it has to be a third generation z pod Mark 77Z with 8 gigabytes or whatever they are and a special video crystal limited issue carrying case. And you know if that's not what they get, there'll be all hell to pay. So I just say – Ho! Ho! Ho! – and leave it at that. Except finally I didn't.

(Pause.)

It all came to head yesterday on Christmas Eve. I was talking to Mohammed the security guard. He's a nice bloke and the only person in the whole centre who doesn't let Christmas get him down. He's still a young bloke but he's got three kids. It's a big responsibility, he said. You want so much to do the best by them. You don't want them to end up like the kids around here, drunk, violent and disrespectful of their elders. I could only nod and agree. Penny and I have always tried to do our best by our Sally.

(Pause.)

And at that point that the dreaded Kevin, manager of the whole shopping centre, came marching up. I don't think he's really that old but he shaves off what's left of his hair to give himself some authority. I thought maybe he was going to have a swipe at Mohammed for talking to me. But it was me he had in his sights. Apparently there'd be a complaint. Some mother said I had been rude to her child. Well, I wasn't going to deny what happened. There was this child, only six but with the build of a Sumo wrestler. And I'd done my usual, "And what do you want for Christmas, son?" and he'd launched into the usual list of super mark 15 this and Dr Who sonic that and somehow I'd had enough of it all. I cut right across his shopping list and said, "Listen, sonny, we don't get everything we want in this life."

(Pause.)

And he stopped and he stared as if he couldn't believe what he was hearing. And he wailed and went running back to his mother who was sitting nearby eating a hamburger and milk shake. I told Kevin the manager I hadn't been rude, I'd just been giving the kid the benefit of my experience. Well, Kevin huffed and puffed and said he'd had other people saying that I often looked miserable and bored and they didn't think that was right for Father Christmas. "Christmas is a time for people to have fun and enjoy themselves. It's your job to make them happy". So happy that they blow money they don't have on all the rubbish in this shopping centre I replied.

(Pause.)

He was so wound up that his veins were bulging with tension. I thought he'd burst. All the people dropping stuff on him and the only person he could take out on was a pensioner dressed as Santa. It was pathetic but I knew he wouldn't sack me. It was Christmas Eve, where was he going to find a replacement Santa to do the Boxing Day shift?

(Pause.)

But then something went. I thought – I've been doing this job too long and I don't want to come back after Christmas. I don't need the money and if I never have to say ho! ho! ho! again in my life, it'll be too soon. So I said I was going. After all, I told him, I've a wife at home and daughter and grandchildren due for Christmas lunch, why am I wasting my time here? Suddenly he was all compliments. We really value your work, don't do this to me, Leonard, I'm sure we can sort something out. You'll be letting the whole centre down and what will the kids think if there's no Santa on Boxing Day? But something had snapped. I told him I was off home to my wife and family. So home I came.

(Pause.)

Well, the clock's just struck seven so it must be Christmas morning now. I've been sitting here dozing since I got back from the centre. Haven't even changed out of my Santa costume.

(Pause.)

So shall I tell you the worst thing about the job? Worse than the greedy kids and the tacky music? It's when you're sitting there under that tree with the music blaring out and the fairy lights flashing and somebody comes up - and they think it's the funniest thing ever - and they say – "Well, Santa, and what are you doing for Christmas? Ho! Ho! Ho!"

(Pause.)

Well, in the past I usually said something sparky back like "Well, since you ask, Santa's Elves and Rudolph the Red-Nosed Reindeer and I are having a gigantic piss-up back in Lapland." But this year I've just smiled weakly and gone Ho! Ho! Ho! If pressed, I always talk as if Penny's alive because I don't want their pity.

(Pause.)

In some way the biggest problem about spending Christmas on your own isn't being on your own. It's being made to feel you've failed, that there's something wrong with you. And there's that pitying tone, "Oh, that must be awful for you." And of course it's even worse when you're supposed to be Santa Claus.

(Pause.)

This year my next door neighbours made their usual invitation. They mean well. God knows what they'd do if I finally accepted. I'm sure they think I'm a miserable ungrateful old git. Well, I suspect that's what I've become. And now I've even stopped the pretence of being a jolly old soul professionally.

(Pause.)

And as for our Sally. Well, Penny and I visited her in Australia once. For Christmas, of course. It was before I started the Santa job. We decided we should go because we'd only met Malcolm briefly before the knot was tied and away she went. We tried not to think too much about why she wanted to put so much distance between us and her. Maybe it was simply that she fell in love with Malcolm and he just happened to live on the other side of the world.

(Pause.)

We never really understood how she could do that to us. But we tried. We sat there downing beers in the sunshine round the Christmas barbie in Adelaide with Malcolm's large, noisy and unpleasant family. Sally was very much one of them. She told us were snobs. We never went again.

(Pause.)

I have a grandchild with a strange name. Like Dorchester or Microchip. Well, actually I'm joking, it's not that odd. He's called Deck. As in chair. He was a babe in arms last time we saw him. He'll be a strapping young man by now. I'll always wonder if the rift didn't play on Penny's mind. We didn't speak about it much. But I do wonder.

(Pause.)

I did think Sally might manage her mum's funeral. She wasn't well, she said. But I think the truth is that she didn't want to come. She'd got her big, noisy, Aussie family and she didn't need boring old us. She wanted sunshine and we were far too much winter for her tastes. Still, a phone call would be nice now and then.

(Pause.)

And just to make my cup run over, Rudolph's been missing for a couple of days now. I asked the neighbours and they haven't seen him either. It's happened before and suddenly he turns up as if nothing's wrong. But maybe his luck's run out this time. I'd even got him some special cat food for Christmas. How daft is that?

(Pause.)

I really ought to move. There's a frozen Christmas dinner somewhere and I haven't defrosted it yet. But I don't want to. I don't want anything. I'm just a tired lonely old man in a nylon Santa costume.

(Pause.)

Hang on. That's the cat flap. Oh my goodness, it's Rudolph. He's got a dead mouse in his mouth. Well, I suppose that counts as a Christmas present of sorts. It's the thought that counts – as Penny used to say. (Softly) Ho ho ho.

END

SOUR BEER

Sour Beer was performed by Nicholas Woodeson.
Radio 4
2003

It was combined with historical commentary to create a programme about the Spanish Armada for the series Soldier, Sailor produced by BBC Bristol.

(The distant sound of a trumpet announcing the start of a voyage. Then a slow steady drum beat.)
(Over this the groans of a man in the grip of a violent fever. The drums fade as he starts to murmur through his fever :)

The tackle and apparel of Her Majesty's ship Elizabeth Jonas. Fore topmast. In good order. Fore puttocks. Decayed. Fore topmast yard. In good order. No, decayed, it was decayed. Fore topmast yard. Decayed. Fore topsail. Half-worn. Falls of the tackles . Decayed. 35 fathoms of rope needed for replacement. (Anxiously) No, not thirty five – thirty fathoms, two-inch rope. Don't stop, Martin. Get yourself through this endless night. Keep on remembering the survey we made before we set sail. Tell yourself - if you can survive to hear the birds at dawn, then you'll know you are going to recover. Rope required for replacement – thirty fathoms, two – (A sudden cry of pain.) God help me, my head burns, my stomach heaves, my sight fails me, God help me – please. Help me to live.

(He struggles to calm himself.)

Where am I? Think, just think. Make a survey. Present - Martin Peasgood, bosun's mate, the Elizabeth Jonas. The place – God only knows. Some God forsaken barn in some God forsaken part of Kent. Still we would have all died back there in the streets of Margate if Lord Howard, the lord admiral himself, had not come ashore and said some sort of lodging must be found for us.

(Another sudden cry of pain.)

Lord Howard knows we have done good service against the Spanish and we should not be left to die. So - they brought us here in carts which bumped and jogged on every inch of the dirt paths they call roads and put us pell-mell in barns and outhouses.

(Pause.)

Item – One low thatched roof above me, roughly made, with gaping holes through which you may glimpse the sky. That is where I will first see the dawn when it comes. Item - A rough mud floor below me covered with stinking bits of straw to lie on.

(Faintly the sounds of groaning men.)

All around me – my shipmates from the Elizabeth Jonas, groaning, crying out, scared, dying. But we have done our duty. The Great Armada has been put to flight. The Antichrist will not have England this time. But who knows? They may come back with renewed forces – and then England will need men like me once again. So I have to live. (A cry of pain) Ah! No – please, God! (With an effort) Keep remembering. Ground tackle and other provisions, Great anchors – four. Sheet anchors – one. Great anchors lost at sea – (Fighting for breath) It's as if it's been dark for ever. How many hours till dawn? (Pause.) Mainmast. Good. Main yard. Good. Maintop – maintop - (A panic) I have forgot its state.

(Suddenly he becomes more animated.)

What's that? (Listens) Who's there? (Trying to call out :) Friend, a moment! Stop! Stop, I beg you. Stop. (Pause) You see we are not all dead men. Will you stay with me a while? (Pause) I cannot hear you, sir. My fever takes away my hearing. But do not go – (Pause) Oh thank you, good sir, thank you.

(Another man groans nearby.)

Others will die but I am destined to live. I may not look much, good sir, lying here in clothes I have worn through many a month on land and sea but I serve as bosun's mate on the Elizabeth Jonas. A noble ship, sir, one of her Majesty's own, the second largest in the fleet, named at Woolwich in honour of her majesty's deliverance from the fury of her enemies. Because she has been miraculously preserved from them just as the prophet Jonas was preserved from the belly of the whale. But for all that the Elizabeth Jonas has never been a lucky ship. Look around you if you doubt it. A goodly portion of her crew lie here in this barn. The ship was struck by a fever before the Spanish fleet had been sighted and we replaced those that died. But the fever burned again more fiercely still and now we are laid low too.

(Pause.)

So - it wasn't the Spanish that did for us, sir, oh no. We feared their galleons and galleasses but we sometimes went to within musket shot before firing our great guns. You have to hold your nerve. You have to wait and wait and think – maybe they will fire before we fire. But orders are orders. We could see the mouths of their cannons – and their soldiers crowded upon the deck ready to board us. But we would not be boarded – they had more men, you see. Instead we stood off and discharged our great shot and spoiled their fine ships, firing three shots to every one of theirs. I saw a ship with blood running from its scuppers. It was a wonderful sharp conflict but, thank God, we had the upper hand. Their ships were like the bears they bait on Bankside. They thrashed about with their powerful paws but we were English mastiffs that could hurt them grievously from afar and were not foolish enough to get within their grip. We drove them like a flock of sheep, our captain said. Pray God they are gone for good.

(A sudden gasp.)

Guns – sixty four in number. Gunners – in number forty. Soldiers – one hundred and fifty. Sailors – including myself – three hundred. Captain, Sir Robert Southwell and others, five hundred in all.

(Pause.)

The sour beer. That's what did for us all. Others will tell you that it was an infection in the pitch in the ship's hull. Every one has their own notions. But I know, sir. The beer brewed at Sandwich went sour, because of the barrels. Nothing displeases mariners more than sour beer. So Lord Howard brought in new beer from Devon to mix with it. But taste how it will, it was still sour if you understand me.

(A gasp of breath.)

A sailor needs his beer, sir. A gallon of it is what we are allowed. God is my witness we need it, sir, when you think of the heat of the battle and the saltiness of the food. But it was sour. We all knew it. And then I started to vomit it up till I could vomit no more. And I got the fever which still burns inside me. And a thirst that nothing can quench. And that's why I'm here – among these dying men.

(The groaning men again.)

No – don't go. Sir. Dawn cannot be far off. I stare above at that hole in the thatch and I wait for the first light. We've not seen a surgeon since we were brought here but I don't put my faith in surgeons. I put it in my inventory. (With an effort:) Beef kettles, one. Fish kettles one. Small kettles one, no, two. (Gasping for breath :) Oh, I've every reason to live, sir. I have a golden future. I am good at what I do. I can keep my head amidst the cannon fire and I can write, sir, so one day I'll be bosun. And then there'll be prize money and good wages and I'll sail the high seas with Drake. So I can't die, you see. (Muttering :) Forestay – two parts worn. Fore pennants – half worn. Runners – decayed and -

(Pause. Someone gives a cry of pain.)

That's my friend, Harry. We're both Londoners and we both went to sea as boys. We've both seen hard years and hard knocks in barks and ships but I've thrived better than he has. I'm the bosun's mate and he's a simple mariner. But he knows my family and I know his. And he's dying a few feet from me and what can I say to him? My voice won't carry across an inch of ground. I'd like to be able to tell him we had a famous victory. We chased the Spanish as far north as Scotland even though we had precious little powder or shot left. Will they come back? Do you know, sir? They may have a trick or two we know nothing of. Are they gone for good?

(Pause.)

I'm sorry, good sir, but I cannot hear you clearly. Are you a Londoner by any chance? There's always great talk of the Devon men and the Cornish men but it's we London men who are the backbone of the fleet. I am a seaman, sir, but when there's no work at sea, like Harry, I work as a Thames waterman. Ply my trade in good weather and bad. If you were in London, good sir, Harry and I would bring you from London to Greenwich in our wherry for eight pence. Against the tide twelve pence. It's a good enough living but I'm not going back to being a waterman again after this. I shall be made a bosun and go after prize ships with Sir Francis Drake.

(A gasp of pain again from MARTIN.)

Main mizzenmast. Condition – good, Main mizzen yard – decayed. Mizzen top – (Pause) I have a sweetheart, sir. We are to be married. She is maidservant to a worthy London merchant and his wife, worthy Protestant folk, who look well upon our match. Bess her name is – like our Queen. If I live, I will marry her, I swear to God. I have not always been a virtuous man, sir, but then how many can truly claim they are? I know the whorehouses of Southwark and some of the whores by more than their names. If you work hard you need relief. How much more so when you have been away at sea for many a month? But Bess shall be an honest woman, I swear.

(Pause. A sudden doubt :)

Are you a preacher, sir? This talk of mine smacks of a confession of the Papist sort. I am a Protestant and I have fought in God's own cause. I love our good English church and its head our Queen and would not see the Papists seize control of our island again. But if God allows me to live, I promise him I will forego my lewd ways and profane language. I will pray more and love only Bess. I have a goodly future ahead of me. I have to live.

(Soft return of the distant rhythmic drum.)

No – do not leave me, sir. Shall I tell you why I am going to live, sir? Can you still hear me? (Pause) No false modesty but I am good at what I do. It is not right that I should return to the river and be a common waterman once more.

(Another gasp for breath.)

You see, when we did the survey of our ship's tackle and apparel, it was not John Woodroffe, the bosun, my master, who did the work. It was me. I knew the gear better than he did. My hand was better than his. My memory was better than his. Is still better than his, even though he did not fall sick with the rest of us. I can become a bosun, maybe more than a bosun. I can take prizes with Drake and come back a rich man.

(Pause.)

But there's more, sir. You see, sir, when we were in the hottest part of the fight and the guns were firing, it was me who kicked the men who were frightened or sick and made them do what they had to do. When we were within musket shot of the Spanish, I was there, God forgive me, urging the men on with every profanity I ever learned on the streets of London. (Another groan.) But God will forgive me because we were fighting the Antichrist. This Armada was sent to destroy our English religion and bring back Papist tyranny. The Queen Elizabeth is our sovereign – has been before I was born – and the future of England depends upon her preservation. I do believe that.

(Pause.)

So - when seamen looked at me in a hangdog way or answered me back, I smote them across the face and told them in no uncertain terms they must do what they have to do. And God will forgive me.

(The drum growing louder now.)

(More bitterly :) If I'd known what I know now, I could have told those cringing cowards they had less to fear by way of death from the Spaniards than from the sour beer. (PAUSE) Runners, decayed, thirty two fathoms, four inch thick. Falls, decayed, thirty five fathoms, three inch thick. Shrouds -

(Pause.)

No, please, sir, don't go. I have to see the dawn. By dawn I will have remembered the whole inventory of the Elizabeth Jonas and I will live for many a year. God is on my side. I have fought for the true religion against those who would restore the old religion and all its evil.

(Pause.)

Are you still there, good sir? Do you still hear me?

(Pause. Faint bird song.)

(Starting to panic :) I can hear the bird song. But I cannot see a chink of day light. I am looking up towards that hole in the roof and I see nothing. Nothing – not even the roof. All is still dark. God help me!

(Raising his voice :)

Good sir, are you there? Are you still listening? Will you take a message to Bess? Will you find out if the Spanish are gone for ever? Will you put in a good word for me with Sir Francis?

(The drum beat still louder.)

Good sir, are you there? Are you there?

(Pause.)

Were you there? I am Martin Peasgood, bosun's mate of the Elizabeth Jonas, destined for greater things. (Pause) Who were you? Were you there?

(The drum beat continues.)

If the birds are singing, the dawn must be coming. But I cannot see the dawn. (Pause) Ship's inventory. Fore topmast. Good. Fore puttocks. Decayed. Fore topmast yard. Good. No, decayed, it was decayed. God, have mercy upon my soul. I have fought the good fight. We have repelled the Antichrist. (Pause) Fore topmast yard. Decayed. Fore topsail. Half-worn. Falls of the tackles . Decayed. 35 fathoms of rope required for replacement. (Pause) God have mercy upon my soul, a poor miserable sinner. (Pause) It was not thirty five fathoms, it was thirty. Thirty fathoms and two inch rope. Two inch. And what of the main shrouds? What state were they?

(Pause. The drum beat fading away.)

God have mercy upon my soul. God have mercy upon my soul. The birds are singing but I see nothing. God have mercy upon my soul. God have mercy upon my soul. God have mercy upon my soul. God have…

(As he continues to pray, the return of the trumpet call announcing the beginning of a voyage.)

END

www.ingramcontent.com/pod-product-compliance
Ingram Content Group UK Ltd.
Pitfield, Milton Keynes, MK11 3LW, UK
UKHW041435180426
11947UKWH00007B/451